Rockets

LITTLE T

The Crown Jewels

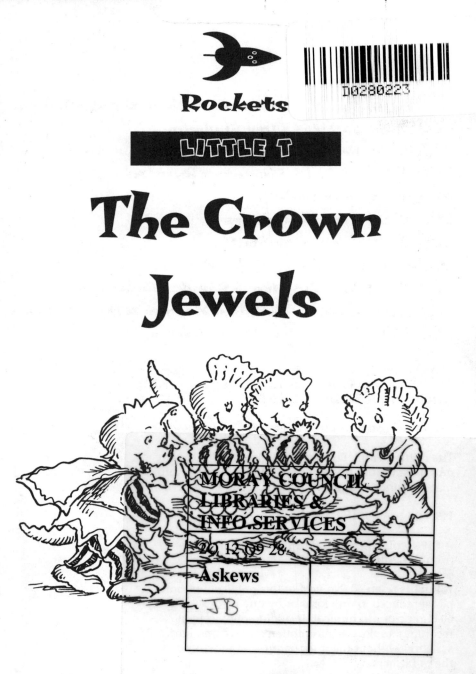

Frank Rodgers

A & C Black • London

Rockets series:

CROOK CATCHERS - Karen Wallace & Judy Brown

HAUNTED MOUSE - Dee Shulman

LITTLE T - Frank Rodgers

MOTLEY'S CREW - Margaret Ryan & Margaret Chamberlain

MR CROC - Frank Rodgers

MRS MAGIC - Wendy Smith

MY FUNNY FAMILY - Colin West

ROVER - Chris Powling & Scoular Anderson

SILLY SAUSAGE - Michaela Morgan & Dee Shulman

WIZARD'S BOY - Scoular Anderson

First paperback edition 2002
First published 2002 in hardback by A & C Black (Publishers) Ltd
37 Soho Square, London W1D 3QZ

Text and illustrations copyright © 2002 Frank Rodgers

The right of Frank Rodgers to be identified as author
and illustrator of this work has been asserted by him
in accordance with the Copyright, Designs and Patents Act 1988.

ISBN 0-7136-6054-6

A CIP catalogue record for this book is available
from the British Library.

Printed and bound by G. Z. Printek, Bilbao, Spain.

Chapter One

Little Prince T Rex was
excited. His mum and dad, Queen
Teena Regina and King High T the
Mighty, were getting ready for a special
dinosaur event.

Every month they dressed in their best royal clothes...

...put on the royal Crown Jewels...

...and paraded through the town.

The parade was called the Royal Swagger.
All the dinosaurs dressed up too and
joined in.

They hired suits
and gowns from
Dinosaur Dress-
hire...

...and had their
horns and tails
decorated at
Dinosaur
Designs.

Everyone looked glamorous... but no one could match the king and queen.
They always looked fabulous.

The Royal Jewels glittered and gleamed...

...and the diamonds on the royal crowns sparkled and flashed so much that the dinosaurs had to wear sunglasses.

But this month the dinosaurs were fed
up. They thought the parade was
becoming a bore.

'It's always the same,' they complained.

And nobody can ever
look as nice as the
king and queen.

True.

The only part the dinosaurs liked was
when the Royal Cook gave everyone a
cake to eat for the parade.

Chapter Two

Little T loved every bit of the Royal Swagger.

'I'll wear the Crown Jewels and lead the Royal Swagger one day, won't I?' he said to his mum and dad.

His mum smiled. 'Of course,' she said.

When you're grown up.

But Little T couldn't wait. He wanted to find out what it was like... now!

So, as his mum and dad got ready, Little T sneaked away...

...and hurried to the Royal Treasure Room.

The Crown Jewels were there, glittering on their royal cushions.

Cool!

Quickly he put them all on... the bracelets, the necklaces, the rings...

...and finally, the two crowns... one on top of the other.

'Phew! These are heavy!' he said. 'But I look amazing!'

Everyone will be surprised!

Everyone was surprised.
The diamonds on the crowns flashed
and sparkled so much that...

FLASH!

...they surprised the
Royal Plumber...

FLASH!

...they surprised the
Royal Gardeners...

...they surprised the
Royal Chambermaid.

FLASH!

Little T was having fun.
As he passed the kitchen door he stopped
and sniffed.

A delicious
smell was
wafting out.

'Mmm!' murmured
Little T, smacking
his lips.

The Royal Cook
is baking the
cakes for the
Royal Swagger!

He looked down into the big kitchen.
Below him was a huge bowl of cake
mixture.
Little T grinned.
'I'll show off the Crown Jewels to the
Royal Cook. He'll be surprised!'

Perhaps he'll give me a cake.

But it was Little T who was surprised.
As he leaned over the rail to look for the
cook the crowns wobbled on his head.

Little T clutched
at them...

The heavy crowns toppled off Little T's head and landed...

PLOP PLOP

...in the huge bowl of cake mixture.

Oh, no!

Just then Little T's dad appeared at the other side of the kitchen.
King High T the Mighty smiled at the Royal Cook.

'The cakes will be ready in time for the Royal Swagger.'

'Mmm, they do smell good,' said High T and began to inspect the kitchen.

Little T backed out of the door in case his dad saw him.

I'll return the jewels and come back for the crowns when Dad has gone.

He turned and dashed away.

When he rushed
back to the kitchen
two minutes later...

...he found another surprise waiting
for him.

The huge bowl of cake
mixture was empty.

Chapter Three

'Where is the cake mixture?' Little T asked the Royal Cook in panic.

'It's all in the cake tins now,' replied the Royal Cook.

And where are the cake tins?

In the oven, of course.

Just then Little T's mum appeared.
'Little T!' she cried. 'What are you doing
here? You should be getting ready for
the parade.'

Little T groaned
and rushed off
once more.

As he dashed back to the
kitchen a few minutes
later he ran straight
into his dad.

High T didn't seem to notice. He was
looking around anxiously.

It's a disaster!

What is,
Dad?

'Your mum and I can't find our special crowns!' replied the king.

'I'm sure I put them back in the Royal Treasure Room last week.'

But they aren't there now!

'The Royal Swagger starts in five minutes and we can't go on parade without them.'

I can't wear this old, everyday crown! It's a disaster!

Little T knew he had to tell his dad what had happened.

Dad... I've got something to tell you.

But High T wouldn't stop fussing. 'Where could they be?' he muttered anxiously, looking around again.

Little T tugged at his dad's sleeve.

Dad!

'No time!' cried High T in panic and ran off muttering.

Just then Little T's friends, Don, Bron, Tops and Dinah arrived.

25

'What's wrong?' asked Bron when she saw Little T's worried face.

Little T told them what had happened.

'The crowns will be baked into the cakes by now,' said Dinah.

But we'll help you look for them, Little T.

You will? Brilliant! Let's go!

As they hurried towards the kitchen Don had a thought.

'It could be easy to find them,' he said.

But when they got to the kitchen their faces fell. It wasn't going to be easy after all.

The kitchen was full of cakes.

The Royal Cook had baked one hundred of them!

Not only that, every one was decorated
with sugar icing in the shape of a crown.

'Oh no!' groaned Little T. 'We'll never
find them now!'

The cook's helpers began to take the
cakes to the waiting dinosaurs.

Chapter Four

Suddenly Little T spotted two special cakes. The Royal Cook always made these for the king and queen.

On top of each one was a wonderful, glistening crown made of sugar icing.

Little T ran to the Royal Cook.
'Can I take the special cakes to Mum
and Dad?' he asked.

The Royal Cook looked doubtful but
nodded slowly.

Only if you're careful, Little T.

I will be.

With his friends' help he carried the
cakes to the front door of the castle.

His mum and dad were there, fretting and fussing.

It was time for the Royal Swagger and their special crowns had still not been found.

'Why have you brought our cakes?' asked High T when Little T arrived.

We don't want our cakes. We want our crowns!

Little T looked
sheepish. He told
his mum and
dad what had
happened.

They looked
stunned.

'So,' began his dad hopefully, 'are our
crowns in those cakes?'

Little T shook his head.

I'm afraid
not, Dad.
I looked.

Little T's mum was puzzled.

So why did you bring the cakes, Little T?

Little T grinned.

For you to wear!

The king and queen gasped.

To wear??

'Yes!' cried Little T. 'The sugar icing crowns are lovely.'

Almost as nice as your special crowns!

High T and Teena looked at the cakes doubtfully.

'They do look very pretty,' said his mum.

I suppose we could try them on.

'Yes!' cried Little T. 'Try them on.'

You'll be surprised!

Chapter Five

And they *were* surprised. Because just as the king and queen gingerly lifted the cakes onto their heads... the castle doors were thrown open.

It was time for the Royal Swagger!

The dinosaurs stood outside with their cakes.

Everyone had sunglasses on as usual to protect them from the dazzling diamonds on the crowns.

But when they saw there was no dazzle they took them off.

The dinosaurs stared at the king and queen.

They stared at each other.

So, one by one, all the dinosaurs put their cakes on their heads too.

But two dinosaurs complained.

They tried to lift the heavy cakes off
their heads...

...but they crumbled in their hands.

From the top of their heads came the
flash of something bright.

The dinosaurs gasped and put on their
sunglasses again.

There, glittering and flashing in the
light were the Royal Crowns.

King High T the Mighty and Queen
Teena Regina were delighted... but they
were also worried.
'How can we explain this to the
dinosaurs?' muttered High T.

I've got an idea!

'All this happened because of me,' said Little T. 'I wanted to find out what it was like to wear the Royal Jewels and lead the parade.'

The king and queen were surprised.
The dinosaurs loved the idea.

Then Queen Teena had an idea.
'Every month from now on will be like a
lucky dip,' she said to the crowd.

The dinosaurs
who find the
Royal Crowns
in their cakes
can wear them
and lead the
parade!

The dinosaurs were thrilled.
'And the rest of us can wear our cakes!'
they cried.

Brilliant!
The Royal
Swagger
is fun
again!

High T grinned.
'Perhaps we should call it the Royal
Cake Walk!' he said and the dinosaurs
laughed.

'Good old High T!' they cheered. 'Good
old Teena Regina!'

Little T's mum and dad were relieved.

'Well done, Little T,' whispered High T.
'To tell you the truth, I was getting a bit
bored with the Royal Swagger.'

But now I'm
really looking
forward to
the next one.

Little T grinned.
'Me too!' he said.

And I'm going to
think of something
to make it even
more fun!